he telling or reading of ghost stories during long, dark, and cold Christmas nights is a yuletide ritual dating back to at least the eighteenth century, and was once as much a part of Christmas tradition as decorating fir trees, feasting on goose, and the singing of carols. During the Victorian era many magazines printed ghost stories specifically for the Christmas season. These "winter tales" didn't necessarily explore Christmas themes. Rather, they were offered as an eerie pleasure to be enjoyed on Christmas eve with the family, adding a supernatural shiver to the seasonal chill.

The tradition remained strong in the British Isles (and her colonies) throughout much of the twentieth century, though in recent years it has been on the wane. Certainly, few people in Canada or the United States seem to know about it any longer. This series of small books seeks to rectify this, to revive a charming custom for the long, dark nights we all know so well here at Christmastime.

THE SUNDIAL

THE SUNDIAL

R.H.MALDEN

A GHOST STORY FOR CHRISTMAS

DESIGNED & DECORATED BY SETH

BIBLIOASIS

he following story came into
my hands by pure chance. I
had wandered into a second-
hand book-shop in the neighbourhood of the Charing Cross Road and
was about to leave it empty-handed. On a
shelf near the door my eye fell upon a copy
of Hacket's *Scrinia Reserata* solidly bound
in leather, which I thought well worth the
few shillings which the proprietor was

willing to accept for it. It is not an easy book to come by, and is of real value to anyone who wants to understand certain aspects of English Church History during the first half of the seventeenth century.

When I opened the book at home a thickish wad of paper fell out. It proved to consist of several sheets of foolscap covered with writing. I have reproduced the contents word for word.

From the look of the paper I judged that it had been there for at least thirty years. The author had not signed it, and there was nothing to indicate to whom the book had belonged. I think I could make a guess at the neighbourhood to which the story relates, and if I am right it should not be difficult to identify the house and discover the name of the tenant. But as he seems to have wished to remain anonymous he shall do so, as far as I am concerned.

The form of the story suggests that he intended to publish it; probably in some magazine. As far as I know it has not been printed before.

I belong to one of the numerous middle-class English families which for several generations have followed various professions, with credit, but without ever attaining any very special distinction. In our own case India could almost claim us as hereditary bondsmen. For more than a century most of our men had made their way there, and had served John Company or the Crown in various capacities. One of my uncles had risen to be Legal Member of the Viceroy's

Council. So when my own time came, to India I went—in the Civil Service—and there I lived for five and twenty years.

My career was neither more nor less adventurous than the average. The routine of my work was occasionally broken by experiences which would sound incredible to an English reader, and therefore need not be set down here. Just before the time came for my retirement a legacy made me a good deal better off than I had had any reason to expect to be. So upon my return to England I found that it would be possible for me to adopt the life of a country gentleman, upon a modest scale, but with the prospect of finding sufficient occupation and amusement.

I was never married, and had been too long out of England to have any very strong ties remaining. I was free to establish myself where I pleased, and the advertisements in the *Field and Country Life* offered houses of every description in every part of the kingdom. After much correspondence, and some fruitless journeys, I came upon one which seemed to satisfy my requirements. It lay about sixty miles north of London upon a main line of railway. That was an important point, as I was a Fellow of both the Asiatic and Historical Societies, and had long looked forward to attending their meetings regularly. As a boy I had known the neighbourhood slightly and had liked it, though it is not generally considered beautiful. There were two packs of hounds within reach, which could be followed with such a stable as I should be able to afford.

The house was an old one. It had been a good deal larger, but part had been battered down during the Civil War, when it was besieged by the Parliamentary troops, and never rebuilt. It belonged to one of the largest landowners in the county, whom I will call Lord Rye. It generally served as the dower-house of the family, but as there was at that moment no dowager Countess, and as Lord Rye himself was a young man, and both his sisters were married, it was not likely to be wanted for some time to come. It had been unoccupied for nearly two years. The last tenant, a retired doctor, had been found dead on the lawn at the bottom of the steps leading up to the garden door. His heart had been in a bad condition for some time past, so that his sudden death was not surprising; but the neighbouring village viewed the incident with some suspicion. One or two of the older people professed to remember traditions of 'trouble' there in former years.

This had made it difficult to get a caretaker, and as Lord Rye was anxious to let again he was willing to take an almost nominal rent. In fact his whole attitude suggested that I was doing him a favour by becoming his tenant. About five hundred acres of shooting generally went with the house, and I was glad to find that I could have them very cheaply.

I moved in at midsummer, and each day made me more and more pleased with my new surroundings.

After my years in India the garden was a particular source of delight to me; but I will not describe it more minutely than is necessary to make what follows intelligible. Behind the house was a good-sized lawn, flanked by shrubbery. On the far side, parallel with the house, ran a splendid yew hedge, nearly fifteen feet high and very thick. It came up to the shrubbery at either end, but was pierced by two archways about thirty yards apart, giving access to the flower garden beyond. Almost in the middle of the lawn was an old tree stump, or what looked like one, some three feet high. Though covered with ivy it was not picturesque, and I told Lord Rye that I should like to take it up. 'Do by all means,' he said, 'I certainly should if I lived here. I believe poor Riley (the last tenant) intended to put a sundial there. I think it would look rather nice, don't you?'

This struck me as a good idea. I ordered a sundial from a well-known firm of heliological experts in Cockspur Street, and ordered the stump to be grubbed up as soon as it arrived.

One morning towards the end of September I woke unrefreshed after a night of troubled dreams. I could not recall them very distinctly, but I had seemed to be trying to lift a very heavy weight of some kind from the ground. But, before I could raise it, an overwhelming terror had taken hold of me—though I could not remember why—and I woke to find my forehead wet with perspiration. Each time I fell asleep again the dream repeated itself with mechanical regularity, though the details did not become any more distinct. So I was heartily glad it had become late enough to get up. The day was wet and chilly. I felt tired and unwell, and was, moreover, depressed by a vague sense of impending disaster. This was accentuated by a feeling that it lay within my power to avert the catastrophe, if only I could discover what it was.

In the afternoon the weather cleared, and I thought that a ride would do me good. I rode fairly hard for some distance, and it was past five o'clock before I had reached my own bounds'-ditch on my way home. At that particular place a small wood ran along the edge of my property for about a quarter of a mile. I was riding slowly down the outside, and was perhaps a hundred yards from the angle where I meant to turn it, when I noticed a man standing at the corner. The light was beginning to fail, and he was so close to the edge of the wood that at first I could not be sure whether it was a human figure, or only an oddly shaped tree stump which I had never noticed before. But when I got a little nearer I saw that my first impression had been correct, and that it was a man. He seemed to be dressed like an ordinary agricultural labourer. He was standing absolutely still and seemed to be looking very intently in my direction. But he was shading his eyes with his hand, so that I could not make out his face. Before I had got close enough to make him out more definitely he turned suddenly and vanished round the corner of the wood. His movements were rapid: but he somehow gave the impression of being deformed, though in what precise respect I could not

tell. Naturally my suspicions were stirred, so I put my horse to a canter. But when we had reached the corner he shied violently, and I had some difficulty in getting him to pass it. When we had got round, the mysterious man was nowhere to be seen. In front and on the left hand lay a very large stubble field, without a vestige of cover of any kind. I could see that he was not crossing it, and unless he had flown he could not have reached the other side.

On the right hand lay the ditch bounding the wood. As is usual in that country it was both wide and deep, and had some two or three feet of mud and water at the bottom. If the man had gone that way he had some very pressing reason for wishing to avoid me: and I could detect no trace of his passage at any point.

So there was nothing to be done but go home, and tell the policeman next day to keep his eyes open for any suspicious strangers. However, no attempts were made upon any of my belongings, and when October came my pheasants did not seem to have been unlawfully diminished.

October that year was stormy, and one Saturday night about the middle of the month it blew a regular gale. I lay awake long listening to the wind, and to all the confused sounds which fill an old house in stormy weather. Twice I seemed to hear footsteps in the passage. Once I could have almost sworn my door was cautiously opened and closed again. When at last I dropped off I was disturbed by a repetition of my former dream. But this time the details were rather more distinct. Again I was trying to lift a heavy weight from the ground: but now I knew that there was something hidden under it. What the concealed object might be I could not tell, but as I worked to bring it to light a feeling began to creep over me that I did not want to see it. This soon deepened into horror at the bare idea of seeing it: though I had still no notion what manner of thing it might be. Yet I could not abandon my task. So presently I found myself in the position of working hard to accomplish what I would have given the world to have left undone. At this point I woke, to find myself shaking with fright, and repeating aloud the apparently meaningless sentence—'If you'll pull, I'll push.'

I did not sleep for the rest of that night. Beside the noise of the storm the prospect of a repetition of that dream was quite enough to keep me awake. To add to my discomfort a verse from Ecclesiastes ran in my head with dismal persistence—'But if a man live many years and rejoice in them all, yet let him remember the days of darkness, for they shall be many.' Days of darkness seemed to be coming upon me now, and my mind was filled with vague alarm.

The next day was fine, and after Church I thought I would see how my fruit trees had fared during the night. The kitchen garden was enclosed by a high brick wall. On the side nearest the house there were two doors, which were always kept locked on Sunday. In the wall opposite was a trap-door, about three feet square, giving on to a rather untidy piece of ground, partly orchard and partly waste. When I had unlocked the door I saw standing by the opposite wall the figure which I had seen at the corner of the wood. His neck was abnormally long, and so malformed that his head lolled sideways on to his right shoulder in a disgusting and almost inhuman fashion. He was bent almost double; and I think he was misshapen in some other respect as well. But of that I could not be certain. He raised his hand with what seemed to be a threatening gesture, then turned, and slipped through the trap-door with remarkable quickness. I was after him immediately, but on reaching the opposite wall received a shock which stopped me like a physical blow. The trap-door was shut and bolted on the inside. I tried to persuade myself that a violent slam might make the bolts shoot, but I knew that that was really impossible. I had to choose between two explanations. Either my visitor was a complete hallucination, or else he possessed the unusual power of being able to bolt a door upon the side on which he himself was not. The latter was upon the whole the more comforting, and—in view of some of my Indian experiences—the more probable, supposition.

After a little hesitation I opened the trap and, as there was nothing to be seen, got through it and went up to the top of the orchard, where the kennels lay. But neither of my dogs would follow the scent. When brought to the spot where his feet must have touched the ground they whined and showed every symptom of alarm. When I let go of their collars they hurried home in a way which showed plainly what they thought of the matter.

This seemed to dispose of the idea of hallucination, and, as before, there was nothing else to be done but await developments as patiently as I could. For the next fortnight nothing remarkable took place. I had my usual health and as near an approach to my usual spirits as could reasonably be expected. I had visitors for part of the time, but no one to whom I should have cared to confide the story at this stage. I was not molested further by day, and my dreams, though varied, were not alarming.

On the morning of the 31st I received a letter announcing that my sundial had been despatched, and it duly arrived in the course of the afternoon. It was heavy, so by the time we had got it out of the rail-way van and on to the lawn it was too late to place it in position that day. The men departed to drink my health, and I turned towards the house. Just as I reached the door I paused. A sensation—familiar to all men who are much alone—had come over me, and I felt as if I were being watched from behind. Usually the feeling can be dispelled by turning round. I did so, but on this occasion the sense that I was not alone merely increased. Of course the lawn was deserted, but I stood looking across it for a few moments, telling myself that I must not let my nerves play me tricks. Then I saw a face detach itself slowly from the darkness of the hedge at one side of the left-hand arch. For a few seconds it hung, horribly poised, in the middle of

the opening like a mask suspended by an invisible thread. Then the body to which it belonged slid into the clear space, and I saw my acquaintance of the wood and kitchen garden, this time sharply outlined against a saffron sky. There could be no mistaking his bowed form and distorted neck, but now his appearance was made additionally abominable by his expression. The yellow sunset light seemed to stream all round him, and showed me features convulsed with fury. He gnashed his teeth and clawed the air with both hands. I have never seen such a picture of impotent rage.

It was more by instinct than by any deliberate courage that I ran straight across the lawn towards him. He was gone in a flash, and when I came through the archway where he had stood he was hurrying down the side of the hedge towards the other. He moved with an odd shuffling gait, and I made sure that I should soon overtake him. But to my surprise I found that I did not gain much. His limping shuffle took him over the ground as fast as I could cover it. In fact, when I reached the point from which I had started I thought I had actually lost a little. When we came round for the second time there was no doubt about it. This was humiliating, but I persevered, relying now on superior stamina. But during the third circuit it suddenly flashed upon me that our positions had become reversed. I was no longer the pursuer. He—it—whatever the creature was, was now chasing me, and the distance between us was diminishing rapidly.

I am not ashamed to admit that my nerve failed completely. I believe I screamed aloud. I ran on stumblingly, helplessly, as one runs in a dream, knowing now that the creature behind was gaining at every stride. How long the chase lasted I do not know, but presently I could hear his irregular footstep close behind me, and a horrible dank breath played about the back of my neck. We were on the side towards the house when I looked up and saw my butler standing at the garden door, with a note in his hand. The sight of his prosaic form seemed to break the spell which had kept me running blindly round and round the hedge. I was almost exhausted, but I tore across the lawn, and fell in a heap at the bottom of the steps.

Parker was an ex-sergeant of Marines, which amounts to saying that he was incapable of surprise and qualified to cope with any practical emergency which could arise. He picked me up, helped me into the house, gave me a tumbler of brandy diluted with soda-water, and fortified himself with another, without saying a word. How much he saw, or what he thought of it, I could never learn, for all subsequent approaches to the question were parried with the evasive skill which seems to be the birthright of all them that go down to the sea in ships. But his general view of the situation is indicated by the fact that he sent for the Rector, not the doctor, and—as I learned afterwards—had a private conference with him before he left the house. Soon afterwards he joined the choir—or in his own phrase 'assisted with the singing in the chancel'—and for many months the village church had no more regular or vocal attendant.

The Rector heard my story gravely, and was by no means disposed to make light of it. Something similar had come his way once before, when he had had the charge of a parish on the Northumbrian Border. He was confident, he said, that no harm could come to me that night, if I remained indoors, and departed to look up some of his authorities on such subjects.

That night was noisy with wind, so the insistent knocking which I seemed to hear during the small hours at the garden-door and ground-floor windows, which were secured with outside shutters, may have had no existence outside my imagination. I had asked Parker to occupy a dressing-room opening out of my bedroom for the night. He seemed very ready to do so, but I do not think that he slept very much either. Early next morning the Rector reappeared, saying that he thought he had got a clue, though it was impossible to say yet how much it might be worth. He had brought with him the first volume of the parish register, and showed me the following note on the inside of the cover:

'October 31st, 1578. On this day Jn. Croxton a Poore Man hanged himself from a Beame within his House. He was a very stubborn Popish Recusant and ye manner of his Death was in accord with his whole Life. He was buried that evening at ye Cross Roades.'

'It is unfortunate,' continued the Rector, 'that we have no sixteenth-century map of the parish. But there is a map of

1759 which marks a hamlet at the cross-roads just outside your gate. The hamlet doesn't exist now—you know that the population hereabouts is much less than it used to be—but it used to be called New Cross. I think that must mean that these particular crossroads are comparatively recent. Now this house is known to have been built between 1596 and 1602. The straight way from Farley to Abbotsholme would lie nearly across its site. I think, therefore, that the Elizabethan Lord Rye diverted the old road when he laid out his grounds. That would also account for the loop which the present road makes'—here he traced its course with his finger on the map which he had brought.

'Now I strongly suspect that your visitor was Mr. Croxton, and that he is buried somewhere in your grounds. If we could find the place I think we could keep him quiet for the future. But I am afraid that there is nothing to guide us.'

At this point Parker came in. 'Beg your pardon, Sir, but Hardman is wishful to speak to you. About that there bollard on the quarterdeck, Sir—stump on the lawn, I should have said, Sir—what you told him to put over the side.'

We went out, and found Hardman and the boy looking at a large hole in the lawn. By the side of it lay what we had taken for a tree stump. But it had never struck root there. It was a very solid wooden stake, some nine feet in length over all, with a sharp point. It had been driven some six feet into the ground, passing through a layer of rubble about three feet from the surface. At the bottom the hole widened, forming a large, and plainly artificial, cavity. The earth here looked as if it had been recently disturbed, but the condition of the stake showed that that was impossible. It was obvious to both of us that we had come upon Mr. Croxton's grave, at the original crossroads, and that what had appeared to be a natural stump was really the stake which had been driven through it to keep him there. We did not, of course, take the gardeners into our confidence, but told them to leave the place for the present as it might contain some interesting antiques—presumably Roman—which we would get out carefully with our own hands.

We soon enlarged the shaft sufficiently to explore the cavity at the bottom. We had naturally expected to find a skeleton, or something of the sort, there, but we were disappointed. We could not discover the slightest vestige of bones or body, or of any dust except that of natural soil. Once while we were working we were startled by a harsh sound like the cry of a night-jar, apparently very close at hand. But whatever it was passed away very quickly, as if the creature which had made it was on the wing, and it was not repeated.

By the Rector's advice we went to the churchyard and brought away sufficient consecrated earth to fill up the cavity. The shaft was filled up, and the sundial securely planted on top of it. The pious mottoes with which it was adorned, according to custom, assumed for the first time a practical significance.

'It not infrequently happens,' said the Rector, 'that those who for any reason have not received full Christian Burial are unable, or unwilling, to remain quiet in their graves, particularly if the interment has been at all carelessly carried out in the first instance. They seem to be particularly active on or about the anniversary of their death in any year. The range of their activities is varied, and it would be difficult to define the nature of the power which animates them, or the source from which it is derived. But I incline to think that it is less their own personality than some force inherent in the earth itself, of which they become the vehicle. With the exception of Vampires (who are altogether sui generis and virtually unknown in this country), they can seldom do much direct physical harm. They operate indirectly by terrifying, but are commonly compelled to stop there. But it is always necessary for them to have free access to their graves. If that is obstructed in any way their power seems to lapse. That is why I think that their vitality is in some way bred of the earth: and I am sure that you won't be troubled with any more visits now.

'Our friend was afraid that your sundial would interfere with his convenience, and I think he was trying to frighten you into leaving the house. Of course, if your heart had been weak he might have disposed of you as he did of your unfortunate predecessor. His projection of himself into your dreams was part of his general plan: I incline to think, however, that it was an error of judgment, as it might have put you on your guard. But I very much doubt whether he could have inflicted any physical injury on you if he had caught you yesterday afternoon.'

'H'm,' said I, 'you might be right there. But I am very glad that I shall never know.'

Next day Parker asked for leave to go to London. He returned with a large picture representing King Solomon issuing directions to a corvée of demons of repellent aspect whom he had (according to a well-known Jewish legend) compelled to labour at the building of the Temple. This he proceeded to affix with drawing-pins to the inside of the pantry door. He called my attention to it particularly, and said that he had got it from a Jew whom he had known in Malta, who had recently opened a branch establishment in the Whitechapel

Road. I ventured to make some comment on the singularity of the subject, but Parker was, as usual, impenetrable. 'Beggin' your pardon, Sir,' he said, 'there's some things what a civilian don't never 'ave no chance of learnin', not even if 'e 'ad the brains for it. I done my twenty-one years in the Service—in *puris naturalibus* all the time as the saying is—and' (pointing to the figure of the King) you may lay to it that that there man knew 'is business.'

 H. Malden (1879-1951) was an Anglican deacon, as well as an editor, a classics scholar, and a writer of ghost stories.

Seth is the cartoonist behind the semi-annual hardback series of books, *Palookaville*.

His comics and drawings have appeared in the *New York Times*, *The Best American Comics*, *The Walrus*, *The New Yorker*, the *Globe and Mail*, and countless other publications. His latest graphic novel, *Clyde Fans* (twenty years in the making), was published in the spring of 2019.

He is the subject of a documentary from the National Film Board of Canada, *Seth's Dominion*.

Seth lives in Guelph, Ontario, with his wife, Tania, and their two cats, in an old house he has named "Inkwell's End."

Publisher's Note: 'The Sundial' was first published in 1943 in
Nine Ghosts.

Library and Archives Canada Cataloguing in Publication

Title: The sundial / R.H. Malden, Seth.
Names: Malden, R. H. (Richard Henry), 1879-1951, author. |
Seth, 1962- illustrator.
Description: Series statement: Christmas ghost stories |
Originally published as part of the collection Nine ghosts:
London, E. Arnold & co., 1943.
Identifiers: Canadiana (print) 20190115890 |
Canadiana (ebook) 20190115920 | ISBN 9781771963138
(softcover) | ISBN 9781771963145 (HTML)
Classification: LCC PR6025.A433 S86 2019 |
DDC 823/.912—dc23

Readied for the press by Daniel Wells
Illustrated and designed by Seth
Proofread by Emily Donaldson
Typeset by Chris Andrechek

PRINTED AND BOUND IN CHINA